FELIX AND ~~~~LY'S
Mini
Adventures

The Wild Garden

Carolina
Knight Ewing

Illustrations by Chris Ewing

ASTERA BOOKS

FOR FINN & ELLIE
Our biggest adventure

Dear Wayne

I saw this and thought of you!

I hope you enjoy reading it :) :)

Lots of love

Aunty Nicky
xxx

CONTENTS

Chapter 1

Tug of War

Everly was pulling with all her strength, as hard as she could. Felix was digging his heels into the muddy grass, sliding along as he started to lose grip. It was a fair fight between them in tug of war.

Everly was only 7 and a quarter and a fair bit shorter than Felix but she made up for it in core strength. Felix, aged 9 and a half, had longer legs and speed but his little sister still beat him in a strength contest. They both huffed and puffed, their hands slipping on the rope and their legs getting covered in mud as they giggled in the Spring rain, having fun in the garden while their parents cooked tea.

"Tea's ready in five minutes." their Dad yelled from the garden door.

"OK!" replied Everly through gritted teeth, determined to win against her big brother.

She caught him off guard as he slipped in a muddy patch and she yanked the rope with all her strength, sending him flying into a big puddle with a yelp.

"I'm the winner!" exclaimed Everly, pleased as punch with herself.

Felix grumbled and groaned as he lay there, winded and muddy, defeated once again by Everly the conqueror. She raised her arms and ran around the garden, a muddy and messy victory lap in what was now pouring rain. At least it would wash the mud off, Felix thought, and he might even skip a bath tonight if he played his cards right.

"Come in you two, you're soaked!" their Mum called from the house, ready with a towel to dry them off before tea.

They'd had a busy day at school and always enjoyed some time in the garden, especially in the Spring when the days were getting longer and the air was warming up. They both devoured their tea and guzzled their juice, ready for a re-match as soon as the rain had stopped.

They grabbed a couple of chewy sweets each on their  way out of the door and got straight back outside, one sweet in their mouths and a spare in their pockets.

"Right!" declared Felix, "It's definitely my turn to beat you."

"No way," grinned Everly, "not a chance! I'm stronger than you." And she was right. Even as a tiny wee girl, as soon as she learnt to walk Everly was clearly a strong kid. She lifted the cat before he quickly wriggled out of her arms, she lifted her cot with one arm and she took great pleasure in lifting the sofa **WITH** her Mum sitting on it as she got older. She was one strong kid.

Felix didn't stand a chance.

His thing was speed. He was a fast runner,

whether in a race, dribbling the ball while

playing   football

or just chasing his friends in the yard at school.

He was also a quick thinker; his brain dashed all

over the place and his thoughts sometimes

jumbled out faster than his mouth could speak. He

was built for speed.

He grabbed one end of the rope and Everly grabbed the other, both bracing themselves for another mudfest and rope burn, both wanting to claim victory and defeat the other.

As they stood there the skies rumbled overhead, another storm brewing and the light quickly failing as the clouds whipped past the sun. The wind howled past their ears, Everly's curls swirling around her face as she gripped the rope with renewed energy and determination.

Just as Felix shouted "3,2,1...Pull!" they both fell backwards in a swirl of light and wind. They were dizzy and confused, like they'd just fallen off a roundabout that was spinning too fast.

"Are you alright?" said Everly, her voice sounding small and distant as Felix sat up, rubbing the mud off his face and blinking quickly.

"I'm fine." he replied. " I'm not sure what just happened but I think the rope snapped." he said, looking down at his hands in the dim evening light.

"I don't think the rope snapped," Everly exclaimed, "I think it grew!" She was right. The coil of rope between them had become as big as a tree trunk and they made their way towards each other over it, carefully clambering over large clumps of sticky mud until they reached the middle.

"Everly, I don't think the rope grew," said Felix slowly. "Look at the trees, look at the grass, look at the garden!" he said more urgently. "I think... I think we've *shrunk!*"

Chapter 2

A Storm Brewing

They sat there in stunned silence for a few seconds
as they took in what had happened. Everly stuck
her hands out and checked that she still had ten
fingers and then looked over to Felix who was
having a good look at himself too.

"You're tiny!" said Everly, gasping as she noticed that his arms looked as thin as matchsticks. "Like a Lego Man!" she continued, amazed at just how small he had got.

"You're not all that big yourself." Felix replied, teasing his sister. Everly looked down at her legs and noticed that even her shoes had shrunk and were as small as tiny doll's shoes. Very muddy, scruffy doll's shoes.

"What happened?" she asked Felix, looking at him with a puzzled expression on her face. "I have no idea." Felix replied. "I'm not sure if it was the wind, the storm...or maybe we were struck by lightning?" he asked.

"I didn't feel any electricity, just a bright light in my eyes and a sudden dizzy spell." explained Everly, trying to get her thoughts straight while her head still spun.

Just as Felix was about to reply, a

HUGE

swishing, splashy, crashing noise made him jump out of his skin and suddenly Everly wasn't on the rope any more.

She'd been splashed by a drop of rain.

Except it wasn't a drop for them, it was a deluge, like someone had dumped a massive bucket of water on her head and sent her flying into the muddy grass below.

Felix jumped down without a second thought; he knew that it was dangerous up there on the rope if the rain got any heavier.

They needed to find shelter.

He grabbed Everly's hand and yanked her onto her feet, her shoes squelching in the sticky mud. He looked around but all he could see were absolutely

MASSIVE

blades of grass

like skyscrapers surrounding them on the

enormous lawn.

"We need to hide under a bush!" he yelled urgently, pointing towards the Willow in the far corner of the lawn that spread its branches low and wide onto the grass, creating a perfect shelter for them from the rain.

What would be three or four steps to them as full size kids was at least an hour's walk for them now. "Let's get a move on." he said firmly.

They kept glancing up at the sky which had turned an ominous shade of grey, the clouds whipping about like candy floss.

At least the wind was doing a good job of keeping most of the rain away so they managed to dodge the few incoming rain drops that fell their way.

Every now and then they'd stop to get their bearings, shimmying

up a blade

of grass

or clambering up a stick, taking turns to spot the willow bush and work out how long it would take them to reach refuge.

They were nearly there when the wind suddenly

dropped and the sky

turned leaden.

The heavens opened,

unleashing massive drops

of rain upon them and they had no choice but to

run as fast as they could.

Felix got a head start

but Everly was right

behind him, puffing

and panting as her

calves ached and her

chest burnt from the effort.

Felix led them the short distance to the safety of the lowest branches and they collapsed in a heap under the leaves and flowers of the goat willow tree, breathing heavily but relieved to finally stop moving.

"We made it." panted Everly, catching her breath and allowing herself a smile of relief.

Chapter 3

Old Willow Tree

They'd been so busy running and dodging that they'd had no time to work out what had just happened to them.

"I can't actually believe we've shrunk!" said Everly, her eyes wide as she took it all in.

"What do we do now?" she asked, looking at her brother with a hint of worry on her face.

"We don't panic." he said calmly. "We work out how we got small and do it in reverse." he reasoned.

"There must have been a trigger and we will work it out. But right now I need something to eat. That was hard work!" he said, glancing around at their surroundings.

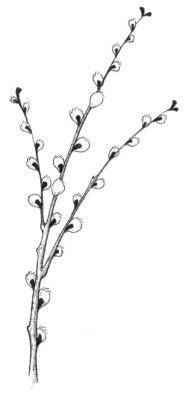

They took a moment to look around properly and they found that the shelter of the Willow was a bit of a maze of branches and flowers, leaves and catkins.

There was something else too, a gentle hum in the background that they couldn't quite place. Felix stuck his hand in his pocket gleefully, remembering that he'd stashed a chewy sweet as he left the house and Everly did the same, delighting in the juiciness of the tiny treat that had shrunk like they had.

It seemed that everything on them had shrunk; their clothes and their sweets but not the rope.

Everything else in the garden remained full size too.

The rain was still lashing down as they sat quietly side by side, taking it all in and enjoying the peaceful shelter of the Willow. After a good 10 minutes of heavy rain it started easing up, just as the sun crept lower in the sky and nightfall was almost upon them.

"It'll be dark soon." said Felix with renewed urgency. "We have to get to the house."

Everly was distracted by the humming sound that had grown louder while Felix was speaking; it was now a buzz, a din above their heads.

A bumble bee had been drawn to the willow flowers, or perhaps their sweet wrappers had also tempted it in.

Either way it was enormous and cast a shadow over them, looming just above the branches that sheltered them. It settled on a willow branch just above their heads and stuck its long tongue-like proboscis out to suck the nectar up.

As it sat there something incredible happened. The bee seemed to be a magnet for the pollen on the willow. It almost sucked it towards itself, drawn like a magnetic charge towards the bee's body. "It's collecting pollen!" whispered Felix quietly, not sure whether to be frightened or in awe of this amazing insect that was at least four times their size, if not bigger.

It sat there for what felt like ages, sucking up all the nectar goodness from the flower, probably making its way back to its nest for the night when it was done.

Everly quietly stretched her hand out to hold her big brother's hand, seeking reassurance from him when usually she was the brave one.

"I don't think it's noticed us." said Felix, squeezing his little sister's hand.

Just as he said that the bee paused and lifted its head, looking directly at them.

"I see you," it said, solemnly, "and I won't hurt you." it continued. "I've seen you in the garden before and you never wave me off, you are kind to have so many bushes flowering for us and you leave delicious dandelions growing on your lawn. We are friends." it finished, turning its attention back to the flowers.

Felix and Everly stood there in awe, mouths open at the talking bumble bee.

Except its mouth didn't move and it didn't seem to make any noise.

It was almost like they heard it inside their heads, like it communicated directly to their minds.

Maybe it was on a different frequency that they could now pick up, Felix wondered to himself, like a radio perhaps.

Whatever the reason, Felix was delighted. He could talk to insects! He took a deep breath and focused his thoughts.

Then he said in his head "Thank you bumble bee, that's very kind of you to say." His parents had taught them both to be polite and he thought this was a good time to start listening to them.

Everly turned and looked at Felix in wonder since she'd heard him too, her mind was also tuned into his even though he hadn't spoken a word.

She remembered that bumble bees don't have ears so she composed her thoughts and looked straight at the bee, directing her mind towards it.

Chapter 4

Bombus the Bumblebee

"I'm Everly," she said in her head, "and that's my brother Felix." she added. "What's your name?" "You can call me Bombus." the bumble bee replied, its voice booming in her head and Felix's too.

"I'm a queen bumble bee collecting pollen and nectar. The goat willow is our favourite tree in early Spring." she continued, "You've made a good choice of shelter. You'll find many friends under here." she finished.

"Thank you very much." said Everly, "it's so nice to meet you." she continued excitedly, warming to the idea of being friends with a bumble bee.

"Let me show you around." said Bombus, flying quickly over to them and taking them by surprise with her speed. She was even bigger up close and they could see every detail of her hairy, stripy body and delicate wings.

She'd already collected some pollen and it was stored in pockets on the sides of her legs, ready to be transported safely back to the nest to feed the new colony that she had to start from scratch every year.

She led the way, guiding them gently up the branches as she flew steadily alongside them, encouraging them further into the mighty goat willow bush and its maze of branches underneath.

Everything looked so detailed and intricate up close; the bark of the branches, the soft, silvery catkins that were as smooth as a cat's fur with

beautiful delicate flowers that were so important to the bumble bees this early in Spring.

"We come here every day," explained Bombus, "and we know all the other insects who live here too. There's a beetle, a few worms that pop up every now and then and there's a hedgehog that walks by at dusk, just out of hibernation and looking for food. The worms always hide when they hear it coming." said Bombus while the kids peered into the dark to see if they could spot anyone.

"There are plenty of slugs and snails hiding under the lowest branches and rocks too." Bombus continued, "They don't come out much during the day," she finished "but it's getting dark soon so you may yet see them."

"Felix! It's getting dark!" said Everly, reminded once again that the garden would soon be pitch black and the walk to the house would be a near impossible mission. "What are we going to do?"

"We need to work out how we became so small," Felix explained to Bombus, "and we need to undo it and become our full sized selves again soon." he said.

"Well," said Bombus and paused to look them straight in the eyes. "Are you sure you want to be big again?" she asked carefully.

"Yes." said Everly firmly, then "Maybe," she continued, unsure all of sudden. "Do you think we can stay small a little longer?" she suddenly thought, starting to imagine all the adventures they could have while this tiny.

"I think we'd be happier if we knew how it happened," reasoned Felix, "and knew how to make ourselves big or small if we wanted to." he elaborated, thinking out loud.

He realised every thought was now shared with everyone around him anyway, there were no secrets when everyone could read his mind.

"I think you'll find the answers you are looking for soon enough," Bombus said enigmatically, "just be patient and stick with me for now. We will make sure you are home safe soon enough." she said reassuringly.

Felix and Everly looked at each other and nodded in agreement. They were both glad to have a trusty guide in the wild garden, come what may.

Chapter 5

The Helicopter Ride

"Listen!" Felix turned all of a sudden. "did you hear that?"

Everly strained her mind away from the willow bush and allowed her thoughts to settle.

Then she heard it clear as day, a word that echoed in her head.

"HELP!"

"Help me, *please*!" came a distant cry.

"Who's that?" asked Felix, peering up to Bombus who was already setting off into the distance. She turned around abruptly and returned to the branch.

"It's the hedgehog." She said. "Jump on my back, it's the quickest way to get to it." she lowered her wings as she spoke. "Hold on tight. It's like riding on top of a helicopter!" she cautioned as they clambered on without a second thought, holding onto her hairs and clamping their legs for grip.

There wasn't much space on her back and they clung together, huddled up as tight as possible. They lowered their heads as her wings started vibrating right behind them, rotating like chopper blades as she lifted into the sky.

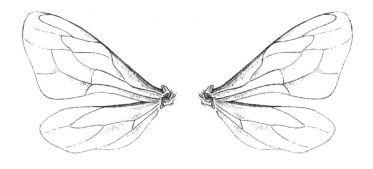

The noise and vibration were deafening but they couldn't cover their ears; they couldn't let go and risk falling off. They looked at each other and couldn't quite believe what was happening.

They were riding on the back of a *bumble bee*!

Things were happening so quickly they hadn't even had a chance to think about it but this was up there with the oddest things that had happened to them, *ever*. The garden looked vast and wild in the fading light and the house in the distance felt like a different planet.

The lights were on in the living room and Everly wondered if their parents had missed them yet. They had been out for over an hour already but it wasn't unusual for them to stay out until dark so maybe Mum would call them in soon and start to

worry if she didn't get an answer back.

Everly's thoughts turned back to the matter at hand

as   Bombus   whizzed   and

swayed

around,

whipped off course

by the wind and struggling with

the extra weight on her back. They were all

thankful that the rain had stopped at least. She was

a fast flyer and Felix remembered reading at

school that bumble bees could fly at speeds upwards of 10 miles an hour, with their wings beating 130 times per second.

He held on as tight as he could as Bombus swung down to the ground, descending to where she thought the hedgehog's nest might be. It was dark now and the street lights in the village switched on, sending a dim ray of light into the bottom of the garden where they found themselves.

They dropped off Bombus' back with a thump and lay there for a second, catching their breath and letting the din in their ears from all the buzzing settle down. What a ride.

Chapter 6

To The Rescue

They both looked around as Bombus took off to
try and get a better view, quickly disappearing into
the dark skies that surrounded her. The sound of
her whirring wings filled the air once again.

The sound of the hedgehog calling wasn't muffled however, and they remembered once again that they were using their newfound skill of mind reading to hear its call.

It didn't help them with working out where the noise was coming from though so they weren't sure precisely where to look. "Tell us exactly where you are." Felix asked, lifting a huge leaf

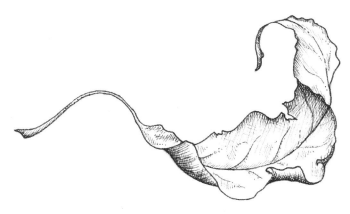

above his head to peer under it.

"I'm under the apple trees," replied the hedgehog, "and I'm *stuck*!" it said with urgency in its voice. "Please come quickly."

Bombus had laid them down on the edge of the main gravel path near the bottom of the garden and thankfully the apple trees were in the patch closest to them.

But, rather unhelpfully, they were on the wrong side of the path. The gravel, to make matters worse, was more like a field of boulders when they were this small.

They made their way carefully over each one, clambering up one side and sliding down the other as they made their way to the other side of the path. It was a slow business, being tiny. Every now and then they slid too fast and crashed into the next gravel rock with a heavy thud that winded them.

"Ouch!" cried Felix as he bashed his leg into yet another massive boulder. It was exhausting work and by the time they got to the edge they had no energy left.

They sat on the wooden edge of the path that was as wide as a bench to them, taking a moment to catch their breath and work out where to go next.

"We're near the trees," Everly called out in her mind. "can you tell us which one you're closest to?" she asked the hedgehog.

"I'm under the middle tree." the hedgehog called back. "Please hurry."

"We're on our way." Everly replied, lifting herself to her feet for one last push to their destination.

No matter how tired they were they knew they needed to help the hedgehog. It sounded so worried and distressed and they just couldn't leave it there all night to fend for itself.

Bombus buzzed far above them as they all searched the area, pushing enormous dried stalks and winter leaves to the side as they steadily made their way through the undergrowth.

Then they saw it up ahead, a huge mass of spikes and big brown eyes looking at them in the dark, its shiny snout just visible.

They quickly saw what the problem was. The hedgehog had encountered a massive bag of crisps and a hole must have been ripped in it, just big enough for its head to go in and not come back out. It formed a necklace around its neck and it was on too tight for the wind to budge. The litter must have been blown in off the road and ended up in the garden.

The hedgehog was in real trouble and needed their help.

Chapter 7

Erin The Hedgehog

Felix and Everly jumped into action.

"You take the right side and I'll take the left." Felix said quickly, working out a plan in his head as he spoke.

The crisp packet was the size of a tent to Felix and Everly and the hedgehog was as big as an elephant. They took it all in and tried to work out what to do next.

It would be a mammoth task to free it.

Everly glanced up at the hedgehog as she walked past its long snout and gave it a kind smile. Everly could see the worry in its eyes and was thankful that she was there to help.

She was also angry that the poor hedgehog had become stuck, angry at the person who had absent-mindedly thrown that crisp packet out of their car window or let it slip from their pocket as they walked past.

The hedgehog was just minding its own business and here it was, in danger all of a sudden and needing their help to get out of trouble.

Everly took a deep breath and focused on the job she had to do. Felix was already positioned at the other side, two hands gripping the edges of the crisp packet as he rolled his shoulders back and gathered his strength.

Everly gripped her side with two firm hands. It was just like tug of war, she told herself. Except the packet was slippery, especially when wet as it was now after the rain, and as they pulled with all their strength they both fell backwards and the packet didn't budge an inch.

This was going to be *tricky.*

"It's too slippery!" Felix called out as the hedgehog looked down in dismay, its brown eyes filled with sadness.

"We need to find something to add some grip." he said.

"I know," said Everly, "we can make holes in it for handles." she thought. "maybe we can use a stick to poke a hole through each end."

"That might just work." Felix replied as he glanced down looking for the right stick. It would have barely been a twig to him if he was full size

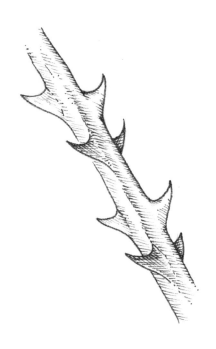

but the problem they had was most of the twigs were now the size of them both combined and too thick for them to even pick up. They scrambled around looking for something small enough for them to handle and eventually Everly found the ideal thing. It was a dried up bramble thorn and it was as sharp as a shark's tooth but it was the right tool for the job.

If she wasn't careful it would also give her a serious cut. She handled it with care, lifting it up with both hands and carrying it back towards the hedgehog.

"What's your name?" she asked the frightened hedgehog, trying to make it feel calm and safe. "I'm Everly."

"My full name is Erinaceous Europaeus, but my friends call me Erin." the hedgehog said. "I live here at the bottom of the garden and I've just come out of hibernation. It's not been a good start to my year." she said sadly.

"Nice to meet you Erin." Everly said cheerfully as she once again approached the crisp packet. "We are going to help you get out of this mess." she continued, trying to keep Erin's spirits up.

"Thank you." Erin replied and Everly turned her attention once more to the glistening packet as she worked out how to use her newfound thorn tool.

She lifted it carefully, well away from the hedgehog's face, and pressed the sharp end firmly down onto the foil packet.

It slipped right out of her hand and she dropped

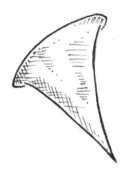 the thorn to the ground, caught off guard by the weight of it. It missed her foot by a cat's whisker.

Close one!

"Felix, I'm going to need your help holding it in place." Everly called out as Felix peered round Erin's long snout. He'd been busy on the other side examining the foil up close and trying to rip it with his tiny bare hands.

Everly's plan was better, he conceded, and made his way round to her side to help her achieve it.

"You hold the foil still and I'll press down on it with the thorn." Everly explained. "We need two holes on each side."

"That might work," Felix replied, "then we can fit an arm in each hole and get a better grip." he said. "If we can then scrumple the edges up a bit it might give us something to hold onto and then pull." he thought it all through, explaining it to himself as much as to the others.

Felix chewed his lip as he concentrated on pulling the edges as tight as he could so that Everly could hold the thorn with two hands.

Her face was a picture of concentration as she lined the tip of the thorn up and then pushed down with all her strength, willing the foil to rip.

It gave way as she strained against it and they cheered in unison, finally some progress was being made.

One down, three to go.

They used the same technique on the three other holes and it took them a while to complete the job, draining Everly of all her strength right when she needed it the most.

She sat down for a moment and Bombus came whirring along, settling alongside her on a leaf.

"You've done a great job so far," Bombus said to Everly, "but your work is not finished yet. Have a sip of nectar." Bombus continued, "it will give you strength."

Bombus showed Everly a leaf with a dip in it that she had used as a bowl, filling it with sweet nectar from a nearby flower for her and Felix to have.

They drank it quickly, slurping and scooping it up with their hands and it filled them with a warm fuzzy feeling, like hot chocolate on a cold Autumn day.

Feeling refreshed, they jumped back up to their feet, ready to take on the second part of the rescue. They would need all the strength they could muster.

Chapter 8

Strong and Powerful

Everly steeled herself as she took up her position on the right side of Erin with Felix on the left. She began scrunching the edges of the foil until she reached the hole she had made and then did the same again for the other hand.

She found solid ground for a foothold with a branch in the right position to keep her feet from slipping in the mud and when she was ready she called out to Felix who was doing the same on the other side.

"Are you ready?" she asked.

"Ready." he called back. "On Three. One, Two, **Three!"**

They both pulled with all their strength and this time their feet held fast and their hands didn't slip, every muscle in their arms straining as the foil stubbornly stayed where it was.

"Keep pulling!" urged Bombus from above, where she was hovering and watching closely, and all of a sudden the foil moved a fraction at the top of the hedgehog's neck.

"It's *moving*!" she said excitedly, buzzing loudly. Everly gritted her teeth and closed her eyes, focused on the slow ripping noise that was coming from above.

Felix let out a yelp as he slipped and fell to the ground, losing his grip once again and tumbling over. It was up to Everly now; Felix had no more energy for a second push, she had to give it everything she had to free Erin.

Everly pulled for what felt like a lifetime and the foil started moving in slow motion towards her, the movement making her open her eyes wide in disbelief.

It was working, the packet was *ripping*!

She took a step backwards and the rip became bigger by the second, the crack widening as she kept backing up with more and more foil in her arms. She was winning.

The hedgehog was straining in discomfort as the foil dug into her neck but she could see that it wouldn't last long.

Erin was nearly free. With one last burst of strength Everly gave it a huge tug and they all heard an almighty rip as Everly fell, half the crisp packet flying over her head and landing in a heap behind her.

Felix, finding energy from deep inside, jumped back to his feet and grabbed the other side of the packet that was still leaning on Erin's face, freeing her from the remains of the litter.

The relief on all their faces and joy at a job well done was clear for them all to see and Erin bowed her head down to them both.

"Thank you for saving me." She said. "Who would have thought that you two, as tiny as twigs, could have done such a thing. Never forget just how strong and powerful you are, no matter how small you might be." Erin concluded as Bombus looked on proudly.

"If you were full size you'd never have heard me call. You've unleashed the power of your minds and now there's nothing you can't do."

Chapter 9

Jax the Cat

"Felix, Everly! It's time to come inside!" their

mother's voice echoed around the dark garden and

made them all jump.

"Everly, we must get back to our full sizes before Mum comes looking for us!" Felix cried, tugging her by the sleeve.

"Can you help us?" he turned to Bombus as he spoke.

"I think there is someone else who may be able to help with that." Bombus said as she flew up high in the sky and out of sight.

"Jax!"

came the call from Bombus, loud and clear in their minds.

"Jax, can you come *quickly.*" Bombus repeated.

"Jax the Cat!" they said in unison, amazed to think that he might be the one to rescue them this time.

A shape started making its way out of the darkness and made them take a step back in awe of the enormous fluffy creature that was quickly heading towards them.

He looked like a mixture of a black panther and polar bear, his black and white fur glistening with water as he made his way through the damp grass of the lawn and into the bottom garden.

"Hi everyone. What have I missed?" he said, delighting Felix and Everly who still hadn't got their heads around the fact that they could talk to the animals.

"Jax! It's great to see you." Felix said with relief, stepping out to greet their beloved pet.

Jax started purring loudly and it sounded like a motorbike was revving in their heads.

He bent down to nuzzle Felix on the nose as he normally did when they were full size. Felix got nudged backwards by the sheer size of Jax's nose and laughed with happiness to see a familiar, but huge, face up close.

"Jax, will you help us get home?" Everly asked, putting a hand up to stroke his fur.

"And do you know anything about how we became so small?" Felix said, "because we need to undo it."

"One thing at a time, Felix." Jax said firmly, "your mother is calling and she will come out to find you any minute now so first things first, let's get you back to the house." he replied.

Erin the hedgehog had made a quiet exit already, unsure of the cat who was quite territorial and keen to chase most animals around the garden, for fun or food depending on his mood.

Bombus was still hovering about.

"It's time to hand you over to Jax and set off to my nest." Bombus said, settling down on the ground next to them. "Jax will take care of you from now on," she concluded. "And we will meet again, I'm sure."

"Thank you Bombus, for everything." Everly said gratefully as Felix nodded his thanks alongside her.

 "Thank you Bombus!" he repeated as she took once again to the skies above them.

"See you again soon." came the words in their heads as they lost sight of her in the dark.

"Right, you two, you'll have to climb up on my back." Jax said, reminding them of the task ahead. The long journey home would be vastly shortened on the back of a cat. What a way to travel.

Chapter 10

Home Time

"Climb up. Don't worry about pulling my fur, you're so tiny. It will only tickle." said Jax as he laid down flat to make it easier for them to get up on his mighty back.

Everly looked at Felix and grinned. She adored Jax and had never imagined in her wildest dreams that she would ever get to ride on his back.

It had been a strange and wonderful adventure and she couldn't believe her luck.

And it wasn't even over yet.

Felix scrambled up behind her and they nestled into the base of Jax's neck, gripping his soft fur as tight as they could to stop themselves from slipping off.

"When we get going I'll build some speed up and there might be a jump or two so hold on tight." cautioned Jax as he sat up, making them grip even tighter. "Are you ready?"

Ready!" they both said.

And with that he took off, leaping over the gravel path and wending his way through the fence that separated the bottom garden from the top.

Their eyes widened in amazement as he galloped across the lawn at top speed, the grass a blur beneath his feet and the wind whipping past their cheeks in the cold night air.

He made it across the lawn in a flash and approached the house carefully.

"I can't go through the cat flap since you'll get pushed off my back." he said, "so I'll have to jump up at the garden door and hope one of your parents lets me in. Hold on!"

Jax stood on his back paws as they held onto his fur, feeling themselves slipping slowly as he stretched his front paws up to scratch at the door.

"Please open the door!" Everly pleaded urgently, "I'm going to fall!"

It felt like a lifetime before the door opened and Jax dropped back down onto all fours.

They saw huge adult legs in front of them, their Mum telling Jax off for being lazy and not using his cat flap.

He ran through her legs and straight to the bottom of the stairs as she opened the door wide and started putting her boots on.

"I'm just going to fetch the kids." she called out to their Dad as Jax jumped up the stairs two at a time.

He pushed the bathroom door open with his nose and they were relieved to finally be in the cosy house; the bath had been filled and the room was warm and welcoming.

They slid off his back with relief and fell in a heap on the bathmat.

"We've only got a few minutes." Jax said, his eyes narrowing as he adjusted to the bright light. "I need to explain a few things to you before your Mum and Dad find you."

Chapter 11

Mystery Solved

"I've been waiting for this day for a very long time." He started, as they strained their necks looking up at their enormous cat. "I was hoping it would come soon and now it's finally happened."

"So you know what happened to us?" Everly asked, eager to hear more.

"All the animals in your garden and indeed the village have known about this for years." Jax said. "We just weren't sure if and when you'd shrink and whether you'd learn to use the power of your minds. You see, it's something you've been handed down by one of your parents and there's no knowing if you'd get it or not until you reached a certain age."

Felix and Everly looked in astonishment at each other as Jax continued his explanation.

"It can happen at any time from the age of 7 onwards and you will unfortunately grow out of it too, at some point. But let's not worry about that for now. Your adventures have just **begun!**" Jax exclaimed.

"So one of our parents could also talk to animals and shrink when they were kids too?" asked Felix. "Was it Mum or Dad?" he continued.

"I think it's Mum." said Everly, "you've always been her favourite pet and she's your favourite grown up." Everly worked out.

"You're right, it was your Mother." Jax explained. "And she talked to the parents and grandparents *and* great-grandparents of all the animals in the area once upon a time. They all knew her well and have told stories of their experiences to their kids so that one day we could tell you all about it too. But she can't speak to us any more. She's a grown up." Jax told them, their eyes wide at the thought of all the adventures their Mum had before them.

"She can't hear me now, or you." Jax finished.

"She'll soon find out that we aren't in the garden."
Felix reminded them both. "So do you know how
we get big again?" he asked.

"That is up to you." Jax said. "You now have it in
you and will learn to control it as time goes by.
You need to concentrate all your thoughts and
think big, or small and you can then go both ways
as you wish." Jax told them. "You will learn to do
it quickly and easily I'm sure, but now you just
need to focus and look into my eyes, take a deep
breath and concentrate."

"I'll go first." Felix said, confident that he could
work it out quickly. He took a few deep breaths

and Jax lay on the ground in front of him, allowing them to come face to face.

He stared into Jax's huge eyes and concentrated with all his might, repeating "think big, think big" in his head over and over.

The words echoed in Everly's head and before she knew it she was saying it too, "think big, think BIG" over and over with her brother and in

the blink of an eye there was another flash of light in her head and there she stood, full size and peering over Jax and Felix.

He was still small.

Everly turned sharply as she heard her mother call, followed by footsteps on the stairs.

"Mum's coming up!" she whispered furiously to Felix, whose concentration had been broken by the sudden panic in his sister's voice.

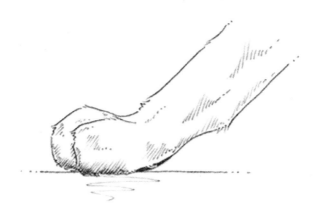

With no time to waste Jax lifted an enormous paw, swiped Felix and tucked him under his furry chin, making sure he was well hidden but careful not to squash him.

"Oh, there you are!" Their mum was at the door, peering into the bright room. "I thought you were still outside." she said, as Everly started taking her muddy shoes off.

"Where's your brother?" Mum asked.

"I think he's in the bedroom." Everly said, thinking quickly.

"With shoes as muddy as yours? I hope not." Their Mum's voice disappeared as she walked down the hall to Felix's room and Felix swiftly came out of his hiding place.

"Quick! There's no time to lose. Let's do it together again and hope it works this time." Felix said.

"Think Big,

Think

BIG!"

And with that there was a whooshing sound and another flash of light and Felix stood before her, full size with not a moment to spare. He'd done it!

Chapter 12

Bedtime

After getting a telling off from their Mum about staying out so late and making a muddy mess in the bathroom, they both got ready for bed in silence as their Mum chatted to them, both distracted and quiet as she asked about their day.

They were too tired to speak as they got their pyjamas on.

A quick bedtime story and they tucked themselves

in, ready to have some time alone with their thoughts and to look back on the wild adventure they'd just had.

Their parents kissed them both goodnight and after hearing them go downstairs Everly waited a few minutes before creeping into Felix's room and sliding in under his covers, top to toe.

"Well, that was a bit of a whirlwind." she said quietly as Felix grinned at her in the dark.

"I can't believe what happened tonight!" he exclaimed and yawned at the same time. "I think we both need to go to sleep and see if we can practice making ourselves little again at the weekend when Mum and Dad aren't watching."

"Good idea," said Everly, "I can't wait! Oh, and we need to get back into the garden to collect all the litter that may have blown in."

"Good night then, see you in the morning." said Felix as his sister made her way back to her own room. He was just starting to nod off when he felt a weight at the bottom of his bed and heard a purr.

He wondered sleepily whether he'd be able to hear Jax's thoughts when he was big?

Just as sleep took over and his eyes got heavy he called out in his head. "Good night Jax."

"Good night Felix." came the reply in the dark.

THE END

Books by this Author

COMING SOON

'The Big City'
is the second book in the
Felix and Everly
Mini Adventures Series.

A school trip to Newcastle is just the beginning of their latest adventure, including a friendly Kittiwake and a

flying visit to St. James' Park where Felix and Everly get an inside view of the famous Newcastle United football ground. Using their incredibly handy shrinking skills and ability to talk to animals, every day is a mini adventure for Felix and Everly.

ASTERA
BOOKS

Quiz Time

N	H	A	W	C	E	F	T	A	C
I	S	B	O	N	X	I	L	E	F
R	L	O	Y	S	P	R	I	N	G
E	S	M	A	L	F	D	L	I	W
U	K	B	S	H	R	I	N	K	Z
E	N	U	B	O	M	E	V	O	A
D	W	S	H	J	R	T	V	Q	U
G	A	R	D	E	N	X	F	E	L

BOMBUS   GARDEN

CAT   SPRING

ERIN   SHRINK

EVERLY   WILD

FELIX

Word Jumble

GEHDGOHE

☐ ☐ ☐ ☐ ☐ ☐ ☐ ☐

SOLMSBO

☐ ☐ ☐ ☐ ☐ ☐ ☐

EBULMEBBE

☐ ☐ ☐ ☐ ☐ ☐ ☐ ☐ ☐

OEWFRL

☐ ☐ ☐ ☐ ☐ ☐

NDAGRE

☐ ☐ ☐ ☐ ☐ ☐

<u>Spring Nature Trail</u>

What can you spot in your garden or local park?

Bee   Cat

Dandelions   Daffodils

Ladybird   Sparrow

Dog   Worm

Robin

Blossom Tree

Add your own sightings too!

<u>Acknowledgements</u>

I owe a huge thank you to Chris, my husband, cover artist, illustrator and sounding board for all the ideas that led to Felix and Everly's Mini Adventures coming to life.

To Louise for the proofreads and moral support, always much appreciated.

And the biggest thanks to our 2 wee sidekicks whose sense of adventure, curiosity and endless questions constantly inspire us both.

Lastly, we owe a huge amount to our pets who I'm sure can talk to us, in their own special way!

About the Author

Carolina Knight Ewing

Felix and Everly's Mini Adventures is my first published work and the series is a door into the big wide world for me, and hopefully my young readers too.

I've travelled a fair bit to far flung places such as Australia, Brazil, Mozambique & Finland and will be taking Felix and Everly to all sorts of exciting destinations too.

But first we start closer to home, in 'The Wild Garden' in Northumberland, followed by 'The Big City' adventure in Newcastle. The North East of England is our home and there is so much inspiration where we live. Keep up with the latest releases and updates on **www.asterabooks.com.**

ASTERA
BOOKS

Printed in Great Britain
by Amazon

79239325R00068